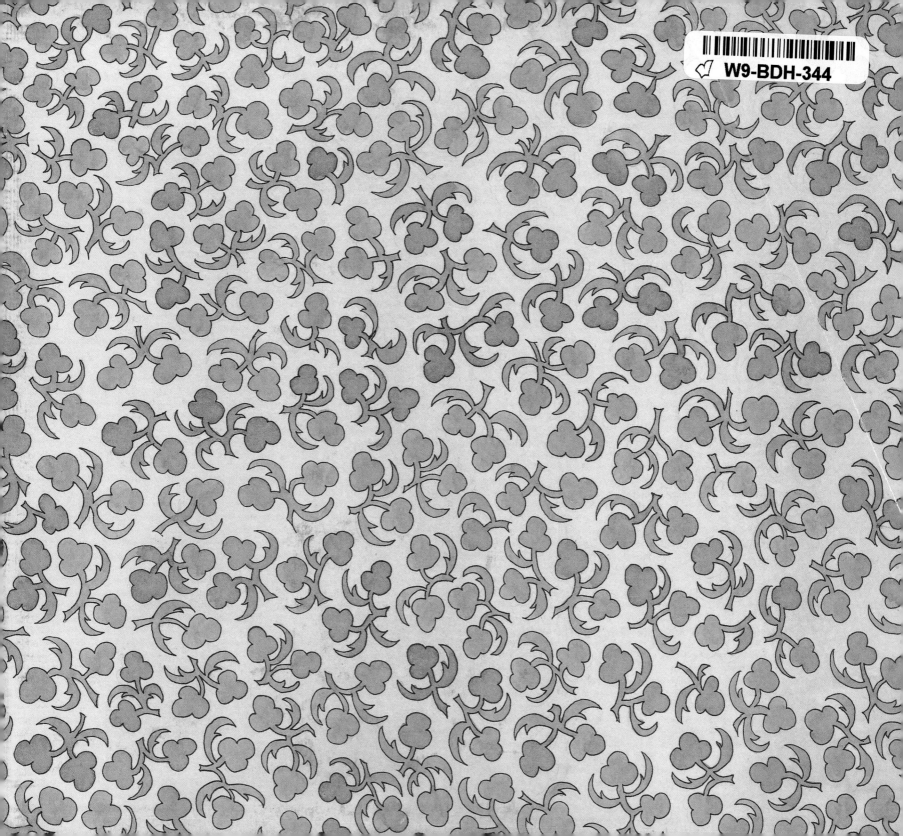

For my sister Martha, whose gentle spirit, kind heart and unconditional love make my life richer.
—S.L.

Illustrations copyright © 1992 by Sylvia Long
All rights reserved.
Book design by Julie Noyes Long & Bradley Crouch
Printed in Hong Kong.

Herford, Oliver, 1863-1935.
   The most timid in the land : a bunny romance / by Oliver
Herford; illustrated by Sylvia Long.
   p. cm.
   Summary : Hoping to preserve peace in his kingdom by
bolstering the natural timidity of his subjects, the king of bunnies
offers his daughter's hand in marriage to the most timid bunny in
the land.
   ISBN 0-87701-862-6
   1. Rabbits-Juvenile poetry. 2. Children's poetry, American.
[1. Rabbits-Poetry. 2. American poetry.} I. Long, Sylvia, ill. II.
Title.
PS3515.E62M64   1992
811'.52-dc20
                                                  91-32536
                                                     CIP
                                                     AC

Distributed in Canada by Raincoast Books,
112 East Third Avenue, Vancouver, B.C. V5T1C8

10 9 8 7 6 5 4 3 2

Chronicle Books
275 Fifth Street
San Francisco, California 94103

THE MOST TIMID IN THE LAND

A Bunny Romance by Oliver Herford
Illustrated by Sylvia Long

Chronicle Books • San Francisco

The Bunnies are a feeble folk
   Whose weakness is their strength.
To shun a gun a Bun will run
   To almost any length.

Now once, when war alarms were rife
   In the ancestral wood
Where the kingdom of the Bunnies
   For centuries had stood,
The king, for fear long peace had made
   His subjects over-bold,
To wake the glorious spirit
   Of timidity of old,
Announced one day he would bestow
   Princess Bunita's hand
On the Bunny who should prove himself
   Most timid in the land.

Next day a proclamation
Was posted in the wood

To the Flower of Timidity,
  The Pick of Bunnyhood:
His Majesty, the Bunny king,
  Commands you to appear
At a tournament — at such a date
  In such and such a year —
Where his Majesty will then bestow
  Princess Bunita's hand
On the Bunny who will prove himself
  Most timid in the land.

Then every timid Bunny's heart
  Swelled with exultant fright
At the thought of doughty deeds of fear
  And prodigies of flight.
For the motto of the Bunnies,
  As perhaps you are aware,
Is "Only the faint-hearted
  Are deserving of the fair."

They fell at once to practicing,
These Bunnies, one and all,
Till some could almost die of fright
To hear a petal fall.

And one enterprising Bunny
Got up a special class
To teach the art of fainting
At your shadow on the grass.

Fainting Class
Today Only

At length—at length—at length
The moment is at hand!
And trembling all from head to foot
A hundred Bunnies stand.

And a hundred Bunny mothers
With anxiety turn gray
Lest their offspring dear
should lose their fear
And linger in the fray.

Never before in Bunny lore
Was such a stirring sight
As when the bugle sounded
To begin the glorious flight!

A hundred Bunnies, like a flash,
　All disappeared from sight
Like arrows from a hundred bows—
　None swerved to left or right.

Some north, some south,

some east, some west,

And none of them, 'tis plain

Till he has gone around the earth

Will e'er be seen again.

It may be in a hundred weeks,
Perchance a hundred years.
Whenever it may be, 't is plain
The one who first appears
Is the one who ran the fastest;
He wins the Princess' hand,
And gains the glorious title of
"Most Timid in the Land."

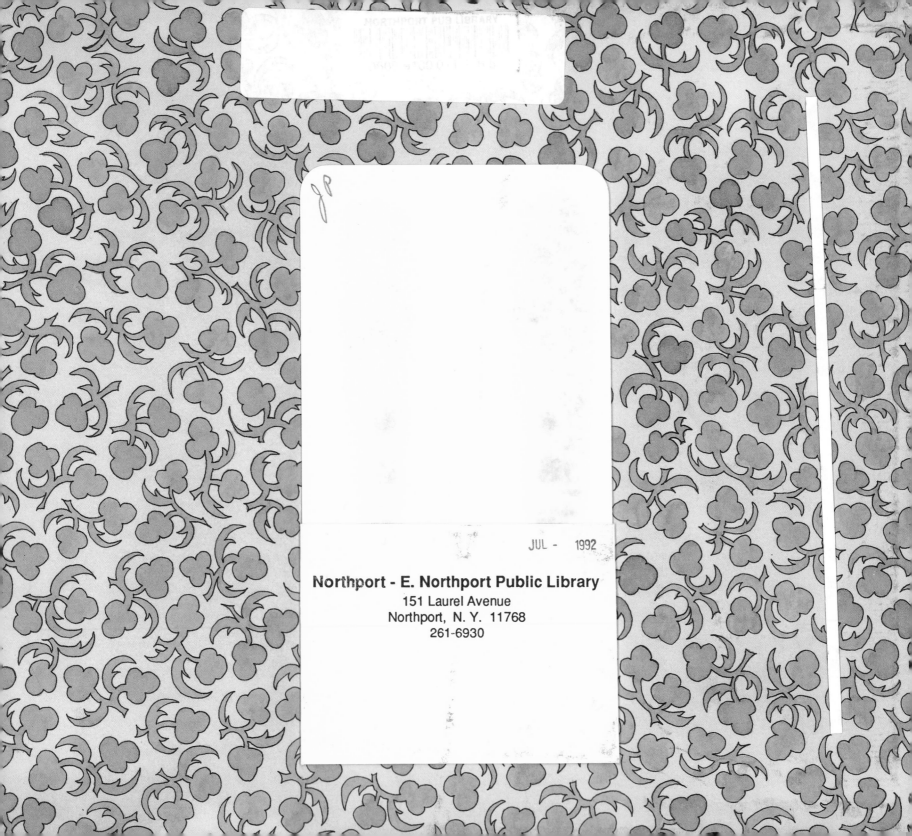